We Are All Born Free is illustrated by:
John Burningham, Niki Daly, Korky Paul, Jane Ray, Marie-Louise Fitzpatrick,
Jan Spivey Gilchrist, Ole Könnecke, Piet Grobler, Fernando Vilela, Polly Dunbar,
Bob Graham, Alan Lee, Hong Sung Dam, Frané Lessac, Sybille Hein,
Marie-Louise Gay, Jessica Souhami, Debi Gliori, Satoshi Kitamura, Gusti,
Catherine and Laurence Anholt, Jackie Morris, Brita Granström, Gilles Rapaport,
Nicholas Allan, Axel Scheffler, Chris Riddell, Marcia Williams

Cover illustration by Peter Sis

We are all Born Free copyright © Amnesty International UK Section 2008
The simplified text of the Universal Declaration of Rights in this book is used
by kind permission of Amnesty International UK Section
Introduction texts copyright © John Boyne and David Tennant 2008
Illustrations copyright © the individual artists as named 2008

First published in Great Britain and in the USA in 2008 by
Frances Lincoln Children's Books, 4 Torriano Mews,
Torriano Avenue, London NW5 2RZ
www.franceslincoln.com

This edition published in Great Britain and in the USA in 2011

A catalogue record for this book is available from the British Library.

ISBN 978-1-84780-151-7

Printed in Singapore by Tien Wah Press (Pte) Ltd. in January 2011

1 3 5 7 9 8 6 4 2

WE ARE ALL BORN FREE

The Universal Declaration of Human Rights in Pictures

F

FRANCES LINCOLN
CHILDREN'S BOOKS

In association with Amnesty International

In January 2006 I published a novel called *The Boy In The Striped Pyjamas*. It was about two nine-year-old boys whose lives change for ever at the outbreak of the Second World War when they are caught up in one of the most horrible crimes that the world has ever seen.

Of course, the war took place before Amnesty International was set up and before the rights listed in this book were written down, so the characters in my story suffered in ways that no one ever should.

I've been lucky enough to talk to children all over the world about my book and whenever I do, I try to explain to them why the characters in my novel were treated so cruelly during those terrible years.

And I always come back to the Universal Declaration of Human Rights, the thirty rules that apply to everyone the world over and not just to those who share our place of birth, our colour or our religion.

Believing in them, acting on them, promising never to break them, that's how we make the world a better place. It's how we make ourselves better people. It's not all that complicated when you think about it, is it?

I hope you enjoy this book.

It might be the most important one that you ever own.

John Boyne

Photo by Kenneth Syle Dundas

I've spent the last three years being part of a television programme called *Doctor Who*. I play a character called The Doctor who travels through time and space in a battered old wooden box. He's 903 years old and he comes from a planet called Gallifrey in the constellation of Kasterborous, but although he couldn't be less human I suspect he's got a copy of the Universal Declaration of Human Rights pinned up in his bedroom in the Tardis. Wherever he goes in the universe, he spends his time rooting out injustice and wrongdoing. He believes that everyone everywhere has the right to be happy and free – just as Amnesty International believes.

When I first heard about Amnesty International I was a teenager, just beginning to take an interest in what was going on in the world and continually shocked at how cruel and selfish human beings could be to each other. Amnesty International represented such a simple idea: that everyone everywhere deserved to be treated fairly.

The Universal Declaration of Human Rights is clear and uncomplicated. It reads like a list of common sense – maybe everyone should have a copy pinned up in their bedroom.

None of us are going to make it to 903 years old, so don't we all deserve to make the most of the time we've got? There are so many of us humans squeezing on to this wee planet and there's no Tardis coming to spirit us away. We need to look after each other.

In this beautiful book you'll find thirty rules for the world to live by.

We're all in it together.

Enjoy.

 David Tennant

We are all born free and equal.
We all have our own thoughts and ideas.
We should all be treated in the same way.

These rights belong to everybody,
whatever our differences.

We all have a right to life

FREEDOM PARK

HELP ME PLEASE

and to live in freedom and safety.

Nobody has any right to
MAKE US A SLAVE

We cannot make
ANYONE ELSE OUR SLAVE

Everyone has the right

to be protected by the law.

THE LAW IS THE SAME FOR EVERYONE.
IT MUST TREAT US ALL FAIRLY.

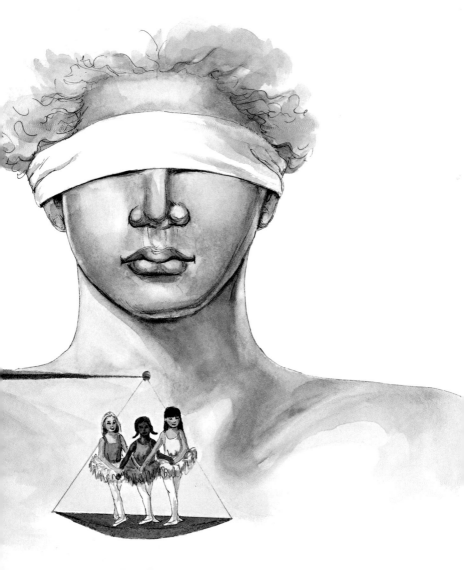

WE CAN ALL ASK FOR THE LAW TO HELP US

WHEN WE ARE NOT TREATED FAIRLY.

Nobody has the right to put us in prison
without a good reason, to keep us there
or to send us away from our country.

If we are put on trial, this should be in public.
The people who try us should not let anyone
tell them what to do.

Nobody should be blamed for doing
something until it is proved.
When people say we did a bad thing
we have the right to show it is not true.

Nobody should try to harm our good name. Nobody has the right to come into our home, open our letters, or bother us, or our family without a good reason.

We all have the right to go

      where we want in our own country

         and to travel abroad as we wish.

If we are frightened of being badly treated in our own country, we all have the right to run away to another country to be safe.

We all have the right to belong to a country.

Every grown up has the right to marry and have a family if they want to.

Men and women have the same rights
when they are married, and when they are separated.

Everyone
has the right
to own things
or share them.
Nobody
should take
our things
from us
without a good reason.

We all have the right to believe in whatever we like,
to have a religion, and to change it if we wish.

We all have the right to meet
our friends and to work together
in peace to defend our rights.
Nobody can make us join a group
if we don't want to.

We all have the right to take part in
the government of our country.
Every grown up should be allowed
to choose their own leaders.

Every grown up has the right to a job,
to a fair wage for their work,
and to join a trade union.

We all have the right
to rest from work
and relax.

We all have the right to a good life.
Mothers and children
and people who are old,
unemployed or disabled
have the right to be cared for.

We all have a right to education and to finish primary school which should be free.

We should be able to learn a career or make use of all our skills.

We all have the right
to our own way of life,
and to enjoy the good things
that science and learning bring.

Nobody can take these rights and freedoms from us.

THE UNIVERSAL DECLARATION

Article 1 – Illustrated by John Burningham

We are all born free and equal. We all have our own thoughts and ideas.
We should all be treated in the same way.

Article 2 – Illustrated by John Burningham

These rights belong to everybody, whatever our differences.

Article 3 – Illustrated by Niki Daly

We all have the right to life, and to live in freedom and safety.

Article 4 – Illustrated by Korky Paul

Nobody has any right to make us a slave. We cannot make anyone else our slave.

Article 5 – Illustrated by Jane Ray

Nobody has any right to hurt us or to torture us.

Article 6 – Illustrated by Marie-Louise Fitzpatrick

Everyone has the right to be protected by the law.

Article 7 – Illustrated by Jan Spivey Gilchrist

The law is the same for everyone. It must treat us all fairly.

Article 8 – Illustrated by Ole Könnecke

We can all ask for the law to help us when we are not treated fairly.

Article 9 – Illustrated by Piet Grobler

Nobody has the right to put us in prison without a good reason, to keep us
there or to send us away from our country.

OF HUMAN RIGHTS SIMPLIFIED VERSION BY AMNESTY INTERNATIONAL

Article 10 – Illustrated by Fernando Vilela

If we are put on trial, this should be in public. The people who try us should not let anyone tell them what to do.

Article 11 – Illustrated by Polly Dunbar

Nobody should be blamed for doing something until it is proved. When people say we did a bad thing we have the right to show it is not true.

Article 12 – Illustrated by Bob Graham

Nobody should try to harm our good name. Nobody has the right to come into our home, open our letters, or bother us or our family without a good reason.

Article 13 – Illustrated by Alan Lee

We all have the right to go where we want in our own country and to travel abroad as we wish.

Article 14 – Illustrated by Hong Sung Dam

If we are frightened of being badly treated in our own country, we all have the right to run away to another country to be safe.

Article 15 – Illustrated by Frané Lessac

We all have the right to belong to a country.

Article 16 – Illustrated by Sybille Hein

Every grown up has the right to marry and have a family if they want to. Men and women have the same rights when they are married, and when they are separated.

Article 17 – Illustrated by Marie-Louise Gay
Everyone has the right to own things or share them. Nobody should take our things from us without a good reason.

Article 18 – Illustrated by Jessica Souhami
We all have the right to believe in whatever we like, to have a religion, and to change it if we wish.

Article 19 – Illustrated by Debi Gliori
We all have the right to make up our own minds, to think what we like, to say what we think, and to share our ideas with other people.

Article 20 – Illustrated by Satoshi Kitamura
We all have the right to meet our friends and to work together in peace to defend our rights. Nobody can make us join a group if we don't want to.

Article 21 – Illustrated by Gusti
We all have the right to take part in the government of our country. Every grown up should be allowed to choose their own leaders.

Article 22 – Illustrated by Catherine and Laurence Anholt
We all have the right to a home, enough money to live on and medical help if we are ill. Music, art, craft, and sport are for everyone to enjoy.

Article 23 – Illustrated by Gilles Rapaport
Every grown up has the right to a job, to a fair wage for their work, and to join a trade union.

Article 24 – Illustrated by Jackie Morris
We all have the right to rest from work and relax.

Article 25 – Illustrated by Brita Granström
We all have the right to a good life. Mothers and children and people
who are old, unemployed or disabled have the right to be cared for.

Article 26 – Illustrated by Nicholas Allan
We all have a right to education and to finish primary school which should be
free. We should be able to learn a career or make use of all our skills.
Our parents have the right to choose how and what we learn. We should learn
about the United Nations and about how to get on with other people
and to respect their rights.

Article 27 – Illustrated by Axel Scheffler
We all have the right to our own way of life, and to enjoy the good things
that science and learning bring.

Article 28 – Illustrated by Chris Riddell
There must be proper order so we can all enjoy rights and
freedoms in our own country and all over the world.

Article 29 – Illustrated by Marcia Williams
We have a duty to other people, and we should protect their rights
and freedoms.

Article 30 – Illustrated by Marcia Williams
Nobody can take these rights and freedoms from us.

We are all born free and equal. Every child and grown-up has rights, no matter who we are or where we live. These rights keep us safe and are part of what makes us human. No one should take them away from us.

On 10 December 1948, the Universal Declaration of Human Rights was created to protect these rights and proclaimed by the United Nations. The world said 'never again' to the horrors of the Second World War and governments everywhere promised to tell people about their rights and do their best to uphold them.

Amnesty International is a movement of ordinary people from around the world who stand up for human rights everywhere. Our 2.8 million members aim to protect people whenever justice, fairness, freedom and truth are threatened.

You can find out more at www.amnesty.org.uk/education

Amnesty International UK
17-15 New Inn Yard
London EC2A 3EA
tel: 020 7033 1500
www.amnesty.org.uk

Amnesty International Canada
(English-speaking)
312 Laurier Avenue East
Ottawa
Ontario K1N 1H9
tel: (613) 744 7667
www.amnesty.ca

Amnesty International USA
5 Penn Plaza, 16th Floor,
New York NY 10001
tel: (212) 807 8400
www.amnestyusa.org

Amnesty International Australia
Locked bag 23,
Broadway,
New South Wales 2007
tel: 1300 300 920
www.amnesty.org.au